EARTHQUAKES
and
VOLCANOES

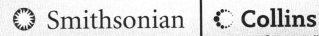 Smithsonian |  Collins
An Imprint of HarperCollinsPublishers

Special thanks to Michael Wise, Geologist/Curator, Department of Mineral Sciences, National Museum of Natural History, and Andrew Johnston, Geographer, National Air and Space Museum, Smithsonian Institution, for their invaluable contributions to this book.

This book was created by **jacob packaged goods LLC** (www.jpgglobal.com):
Written by: Melissa Stewart
Creative: Ellen Jacob, Kirk Cheyfitz, Dawn Camner, Carolyn Jackson, Nicolas Medina
The title page photo shows lava venting and proceeding downslope as a lava flow.

Photo credits: **pages 8 inset, 43 inset, 44 inset, 51 inset, 52 insets, 62 inset, 63 inset, 70–71:** USGS; **pages 1, 28, 38–39, 58–59:** © Phil Degginger/Dembinsky Photo Associates; **pages 54 inset left, 66 inset:** NPS; **pages 2–3 20–21:** Suzanne Plunkett/AP Images; **pages 4–5:** Jack Smith/AP Images; **pages 6–7:** Gemunu Amarasinghe/AP Images; **page 7 inset:** Apichart Weerawong/AP Images; **pages 8–9:** © Martin Withers/Dembinsky Photo Associates; **pages 10–11:** John McConnico/AP Images; **page 12:** © Phil Degginger/Carnegie Collection/Dembinsky Photo Associates; **pages 14–15:** Ed Wray/AP Images; **page 16:** University of Colorado/USGS; **page 18:** Murad Sezer/AP Images; **page 19:** Manish Swarup/AP Images; **page 22 inset:** University of California, Berkeley/NGDC; **pages 22–23:** © Wesley Bocxe/Photo Researchers, Inc.; **page 23 inset:** Washington Dept. of Transportation/USGS; **page 24:** © Oddur Sigurdsson, National Energy Authority, Iceland; **page 24 inset:** © John M. Watson; **pages 26–27:** © Marli Miller; **page 27 inset:** © Bill Lea/Dembinsky Photo Associates; **page 28 inset:** E. V. Leyendecker/USGS; **page 29:** D. Perkins/USGS; **page 30:** © Russell Curtis/Photo Researchers, Inc.; **pages 32–33:** photo courtesy of Transamerica Insurance and Investment Group; **page 34:** Chip Clark/National Museum of Natural History; **page 36, inset left:** Department of Natural Resources, State of Washington/USGS; **inset right:** © Dennis Flaherty/Photo Researchers, Inc.; **page 40, inset top:** Yount/USGS; **bottom:** University of Colorado, Boulder/USGS; **pages 40–41:** Juan Carlos Rojas/AP Images; **pages 42–43:** E. R. Degginger/Dembinsky Photo Associates; **pages 44–45:** Nelson Salting/AP Images; **page 45 inset:** C. Heliker/USGS; **page 47:** David Jordan/AP Images; **page 48 inset:** P. Hedervari, National Geophysical Data Center; **pages 48–49:** Bullit Marquez/AP Images; **page 50 inset:** J. P. Lockwood/USGS; **pages 50–51:** © W. K. Fletcher/Photo Researchers, Inc.; **pages 52–53:** Lyn Topinka/USGS; **pages 54–55, top:** Japan Coast Guard/AP Images; **bottom right:** KenMcGee/USGS; **page 56 inset:** © B. Murton/Southampton Oceanography Centre/Photo Researchers, Inc.; **pages 56–57:** © M-Sat Ltd/Photo Researchers, Inc.; **page 58:** © Sandra Nykerk/Dembinsky Photo Associates; **inset:** NASA/Dembinsky Photo Associates; **pages 60–61:** © Rob Stapleton/Dembinsky Photo Associates; **pages 62–63:** © George Holton/Photo Researchers, Inc.; **pages 64–65:** AP Images; **page 65 inset:** Gerard Fairley; **pages 66–67:** © Dirk Wiersma/Photo Researchers, Inc.; **pages 68–69:** W. Chadwick/USGS; **page 70 inset:** Yonda Sisko/AP Images; **pages 72–73:** NASA; **page 74:** Andrew Johnston.
Maps on **pages 9, 10, 13, 21, 25, 26, 38 inset, 55, 60:** Brad McMahon.

Library of Congress Cataloging-in-Publication Data
Earthquakes and volcanoes / [Melissa Stewart].—1st ed.   p.   cm.   Includes index.
ISBN 978-0-06-089950-9 (pbk. bdg.) — ISBN 978-0-06-089951-6 (trade bdg.)
1. Earthquakes—Juvenile literature. 2. Volcanoes—Juvenile literature. I. Title.
QE521.3.S739 2008   2007002900
551.22—dc22

1 2 3 4 5 6 7 8 9 10
❖
First Edition

SMITHSONIAN MISSION STATEMENT

For more than 160 years, the Smithsonian has remained true to its mission, "the increase and diffusion of knowledge." Today the Smithsonian is not only the world's largest provider of museum experiences supported by authoritative scholarship in science, history, and the arts but also an international leader in scientific research and exploration. The Smithsonian offers the world a picture of America, and America a picture of the world.

Destruction to the island of Nias, Indonesia, caused by the March 28, 2005 (11:09:36 p.m. local time) aftershock of the 2004 Indian Ocean earthquake.

Contents

Mount St. Helens, in Washington State, had a major eruption on May 18, 1980.

A Deadly Disaster

Water sweeps through the village of Maddampegama, Sri Lanka, driven by the tsunami associated with the December 26, 2004 Indian Ocean earthquake.

A giant tsunami struck Nam Khem, Thailand, leaving behind this pile of debris.

In December 2004, as families across North America celebrated the winter holidays, people in sunny Southeast Asia were about to face one of the deadliest disasters in history—and they didn't even know it.

Just a few miles north of Simeulue, a tiny island in the Indian Ocean near Sumatra, Indonesia, a large **fault** under the seafloor began to slip and grind, causing one of the most powerful and most widespread **earthquakes** ever recorded. Earthquakes usually last only a few seconds, but this one continued for nearly 10 minutes. As a huge piece of the seafloor shifted and moved, the ocean above it sloshed back and forth. A powerful **tsunami** formed.

In as little as 15 minutes, huge waves began crashing onto nearby shores. Within a few hours, the tsunami had reached Indonesia, Sri Lanka, Thailand, and south-ern India. Wherever it struck, the tsunami destroyed everything in its path. Experts believe it killed as many as 283,000 people and injured another 125,000 people. An estimated 1.5 million people lost their homes.

What caused the 2004 Indian Ocean earthquake and the resulting tsunami? Forces deep inside our planet are responsible for most earthquakes. The ground below our feet may seem steady and stable, but it's not. Earth's surface and the materials inside are always on the move.

That's Incredible!

The 2004 Indian Ocean earthquake was so powerful that scientists all over the world could detect its vibrations for several months afterward. The tsunami affected areas more than 5,000 miles away from the site of the earthquake. About 16 hours after the quake, powerful waves crashed onto the shores of South Africa.

Layers of Earth

Most of our planet is made of rock. Even the soil you dig is made of broken-up rock mixed with rotting plant and animal material. Dig deeper, and you'll eventually hit solid rock. The soil and hard rock beneath it make up Earth's **crust**.

Below the crust is a thicker layer called the **mantle**. Parts of the mantle are made of molten rock called **magma**. Like cooked oatmeal, magma is thick but it can flow. The material that makes up Earth's mantle is constantly on the move. As the hottest material slowly rises toward Earth's surface, cooler material sinks down to take its place. It may take millions of years for the material to complete one loop.

The mantle surrounds Earth's sizzling-hot **core**. The melted metals in the outer core are at least 6,700 degrees Fahrenheit. The inner core is even hotter, but it is made of solid metals. The weight of the overlying layers presses down on the inner core. All that pressure holds the inner core's molecules so close together that they can't turn into a liquid.

These scientists are collecting freshly fallen ash from a recent volcanic eruption. The ash holds clues about the source of the eruption and the chemistry of the magma.

Beneath the Surface

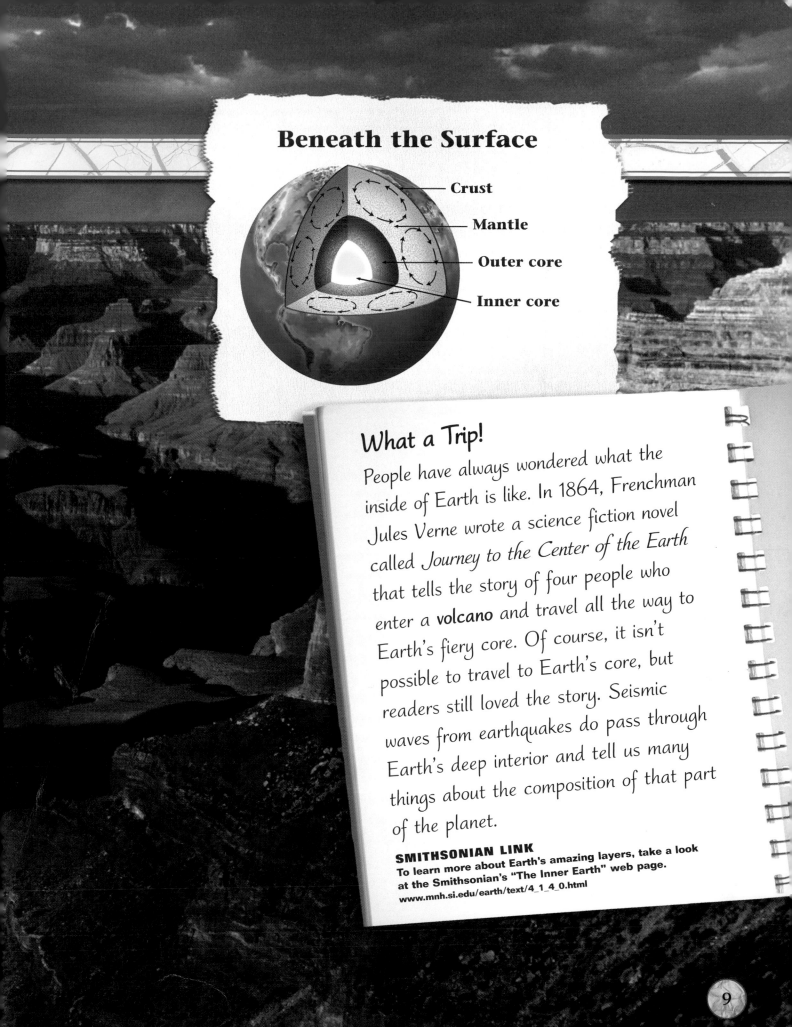

- Crust
- Mantle
- Outer core
- Inner core

What a Trip!

People have always wondered what the inside of Earth is like. In 1864, Frenchman Jules Verne wrote a science fiction novel called *Journey to the Center of the Earth* that tells the story of four people who enter a **volcano** and travel all the way to Earth's fiery core. Of course, it isn't possible to travel to Earth's core, but readers still loved the story. Seismic waves from earthquakes do pass through Earth's deep interior and tell us many things about the composition of that part of the planet.

SMITHSONIAN LINK
To learn more about Earth's amazing layers, take a look at the Smithsonian's "The Inner Earth" web page.
www.mnh.si.edu/earth/text/4_1_4_0.html

Land on the Move

Earth's crust is broken into slabs of rock, or **plates**, that float on top of the mantle. As the mantle slowly circulates, the plates move across the surface of our planet. On average, Earth's plates move less than an inch each year. Your fingernails grow at about the same rate.

In some parts of the world, plates move apart and create gaps called **rifts**. Magma slowly flows out of the mantle through these rifts. It cools and hardens to form new land or seafloor on either side of the rift. As the Mid-Atlantic Ridge, a rift in the middle of the Atlantic Ocean, widens, North America and Europe slowly move farther apart.

Earth's surface is broken into many plates. Only the major ones are labeled on this diagram. The plates are constantly moving in the direction of the arrows. The Mid-Atlantic Ridge is a rift formed as plates move apart.

In other parts of the world, plates crash into one another. Sometimes one plate slides over another. When two plates hit head-on and push against each other with great force, the land buckles and mountains form. As India crashes into the rest of Asia, the Himalaya mountains are slowly rising into the sky.

Mt. Everest (far left) reaches 29,035 feet on the border of Nepal and Tibet. The current summit elevation is 7 feet higher than it was when measured in 1999.

What a Discovery!

In 1912, a German scientist named Alfred Wegener looked at a world map and noticed that if he could pick up the continents and move them, the eastern edge of South America would fit together with the western edge of Africa, just like pieces of a puzzle. Based on this and other evidence, Wegener suggested that Earth's crust is made of moving plates and, over time, the continents have slowly shifted from one place to another. Scientists couldn't imagine what could cause land to move, so many researchers rejected Wegener's theory. Now we know that Wegener was right.

SMITHSONIAN LINK
Want to learn more about Earth's plates and their movements? Take a look at the Smithsonian's "This Dynamic Planet" web page.
www.minerals.si.edu/earth/text/4_1_2_0.html

Fossils Tell Tales

How do scientists know where landmasses were millions of years ago? Important clues come from fossils. Scientists have found fossils of the swimming reptile *Mesosaurus* in southern Africa and in South America. Because *Mesosaurus* lived in freshwater, it couldn't swim all the way across the Atlantic Ocean. So it must have evolved before the ocean formed, when Africa and South America were still connected. Fossils like *Mesosaurus* helped scientists understand that continents could move.

This mesosaur fossil was found near São Paulo, Brazil.

SMITHSONIAN LINK
Find out more about how Earth has changed over time at the Smithsonian's "Ancient Continents" web page.
www.mnh.si.edu/earth/text/4_1_3_0.html

How Earth Has Changed

Scientists have established that Earth formed about 4.6 billion years ago. At first, the entire planet was made of molten magma. It took millions of years for Earth to cool enough for its crust to harden.

Even then, our planet didn't look the way it does today. The continents we see when we look at a map or globe have existed only for about 65 million years. Before that, the land was in different places. As Earth's plates have moved, so have the land and oceans.

Scientists are still trying to figure out all the ways Earth has changed over time. They think that about 1.1 billion years ago Earth had one large continent they call Rodinia. The center of Rodinia was close to the South Pole.

About 750 million years ago, Rodinia broke into three large pieces, and the land drifted north. Then, about 225 million years ago, all of Earth's land formed another giant continent scientists call Pangaea.

As time passed, the plates below Pangaea moved apart and the land broke into two continents—Laurasia and Gondwanaland. As more time passed, the plates continued to travel across Earth's surface, forming the continents we know today.

The continents are still on the move. Perhaps one day all of Earth's land will come together again and form another giant continent.

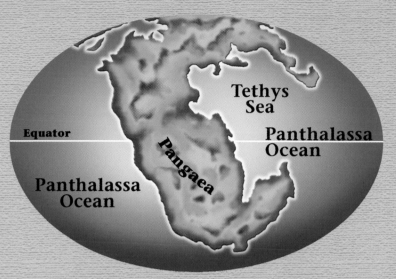

250 million years ago

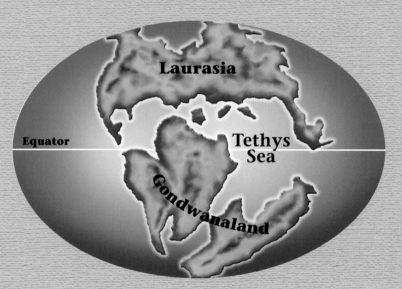

180 million years ago

Today

The Earth Moves

These children are playing along the shore of Simeulue just two months after the 2004 Indian Ocean earthquake. Even though Simeulue was the closest area of land to the earthquake's focus, it suffered little damage from the resulting tsunami.

What Is an Earthquake?

As Earth's plates move, the rocks in the crust get pushed and pulled, scraped and jostled. Over time, strain slowly builds up inside the rocks. When they can't take it anymore, the rocks suddenly crack and shift. Their movement releases waves of energy called an earthquake. The ground shakes up and down and from side to side as energy waves, or vibrations, radiate in every direction. They move like the ripples that form on the surface of a pond when you toss in a pebble.

The point where earthquake waves begin—the place where rocks crack or shift—is called the **focus**, or hypocenter. The point on Earth's surface directly above the focus is called the **epicenter**. During an earthquake, the strongest waves occur at the epicenter; and as the waves spread out, they decrease.

Scientists have identified numerous types of waves that occur during an earthquake. Waves that travel through the earth are called primary waves (P waves) and secondary waves (S waves). P waves travel fast and arrive first at a seismic station. P waves push and pull through rocks or liquids, alternating compressions and expansions similar to an accordion being opened and closed. S waves are much slower and travel only through rock. They cause the earth to shake up and down, causing what would be a small square of earth to become a parallelogram.

There are two kinds of surface waves. Love waves are the fastest surface waves and move the earth from side to side, the way a slithering snake moves. Rayleigh waves roll along the surface, simultaneously moving the earth up and down and side to side.

Did You Know?

The 2004 Indian Ocean earthquake released enough energy to power all the homes and businesses in the United States for three days. Unfortunately, we don't know a way to capture that energy and make it useful instead of destructive.

Size and Strength

Imagine that you are lying on your bed reading a book. Suddenly you feel the bed move. A hanging plant in front of the window swings back and forth, and some toys fall off your shelves. What's going on? You are experiencing a minor earthquake.

More than one million earthquakes shake our planet every year, but most pass unnoticed. About ten thousand cause some minor damage, but in a typical year only two or three cause major destruction.

The strength of an earthquake can be measured by its magnitude, or the amount of energy it releases, and its intensity, or how people experience the earthquake and the amount of damage it causes. A well-known scale that measures an earthquake's intensity is the Mercalli scale. The Richter scale and the more widely used moment magnitude scale both measure the magnitude of earthquakes.

The table on the opposite page shows how the magnitude and the intensity of earthquakes are related. Since the development of these scales, engineers and architects have devised ways to make structures such as bridges and buildings more resistant to earthquakes.

In 1964, a terrible earthquake struck the Prince William Sound area of Alaska. The magnitude was reported as a 9.2.

The 1964 Prince William Sound earthquake caused a major landslide as well as a tsunami. The resulting tsunami severely damaged many boats and washed them ashore.

Comparing the Magnitude and Intensity Scales

Magnitude Scale (Moment Magnitude, Richter)	Intensity Scale (Mercalli)	Effects in Nearby Settlements
1.0–2.0	I	I. Shaking is rarely felt by people.
2.0–3.0	II	II. Only people at rest feel the shaking, especially if they are on the upper floors of a building.
3.0–4.0	III	III. Many people indoors feel the shaking, but most people do not recognize it as an earthquake.
4.0	IV	IV. Most people indoors and some outdoors notice the shaking. Dishes, windows, and doors rattle. Walls creak. Parked cars rock.
4.0–5.0	V	V. Felt by almost everyone. Many sleeping people wake up. Liquid splashes out of glasses. Small objects are knocked over. Some dishes and windows break.
5.0–6.0	VI	VI. Felt by all. People have trouble walking. Some heavy furniture moves. Dishes break, and pictures fall off walls. No damage to buildings.
6.0	VII	VII. People have trouble standing. Furniture breaks. Plaster and bricks may crack and fall. Noticeable waves on ponds. Church bells ring. Considerable damage to poorly built buildings.
6.0–7.0	VIII	VIII. People have trouble driving cars. Walls, chimneys, and tree branches break and fall. Some poorly built buildings may collapse. Tall structures may twist and fall.
7.0	IX	IX. People panic. Underground pipes may break, and well-built buildings are considerably damaged. The ground may crack.
7.0–8.0	X	X. The ground cracks. Water splashes over the banks of rivers and canals. Railroad tracks bend.
8.0	XI	XI. Highways, railroad tracks, bridges, and underground pipelines are destroyed. Most buildings collapse. Large cracks appear in the ground.
8.0 or greater	XII	XII. Destruction of buildings and transportation systems. Almost everything is destroyed. The surface of the ground moves in waves or ripples. The ground is covered with cracks and holes.

Incredible Earthquakes

The 2004 Indian Ocean earthquake was the fourth most powerful earthquake since 1900. The tsunami it caused made it the second deadliest on record. Scientists gave it a value of 9.1 on the moment magnitude scale, but since the epicenter was on the ocean floor, the earthquake did not receive a score on the Mercalli scale.

Seven other earthquakes have been assigned magnitudes around 9 or more. But none of them is among the deadliest earthquakes in history. Some of the world's worst earthquakes occurred before the Richter scale or modern instruments were invented. There was no way to measure their magnitude exactly. Today scientists sometimes use historical records to estimate the magnitude of earthquakes that happened centuries ago.

More recently, some of the most destructive earthquakes had magnitudes around 7. Why did these weaker earthquakes cause so much damage and death? Partly because their epicenters were in or close to large cities, such as Tangshan, China; Tokyo, Japan; and Ashgabat, Turkmenistan.

SMITHSONIAN LINK
To learn more about earthquakes, click on some of the great links on this web page.
www.stcms.si.edu/ce/earthquakes.htm

Following two devastating earthquakes in 1999, many people in northwestern Turkey were left homeless and had to live in tent camps. This photo shows children leaving their tent school at lunchtime.

The Ten Deadliest Earthquakes in Recorded History

Location	Number of People Killed	Magnitude	Date A.D.
Shanxi, China	830,000	8	1556
Off the coast of Sumatra	283,000	9.1	2004
Tangshan, China	255,000	7.5	1976
Aleppo, Syria	230,000	Unknown	1138
Damghan, Iran	200,000	Unknown	856
Haiyuan, Ningxia, China	200,000	7.8	1920
Ardabil, Iran	150,000	Unknown	893
Kanto, Japan	143,000	7.9	1923
Ashgabat, Turkmenistan	110,000	7.3	1948
Chihli, China	100,000	Unknown	1290

In this photo, residents of a small village in India walk past a crack that formed following an October 2005 earthquake. The quake, which had a magnitude of 7.6, devastated the nearby city of Srinagar and killed more than 30,000 people.

After an Earthquake

On March 28, 2005, an aftershock of the 2004 Indian Ocean earthquake struck the island of Nias, Indonesia. It killed hundreds of people, caused landslides, and leveled most of the buildings in the center of Gunung Sitoli.

That's Incredible!

Following an 8.1 magnitude earthquake in New Madrid, Missouri, in 1811, aftershocks continued for more than a year. During that time, the town's landscape was dramatically altered.

Rivers changed their courses, flooding fields and forests. The land became cracked and full of holes. Most of the people living in New Madrid had to move to other places.

The Tremors Continue

The earthquakes that follow a large earthquake are called aftershocks. Within a few days of the December 26, 2004 Indian Ocean earthquake, scientists detected many aftershocks off the coast of Sumatra and in the nearby Andaman and Nicobar islands.

When a major earthquake occurs, the aftershocks can continue for weeks or even months. The largest aftershock of the 2004 Indian Ocean earthquake occurred in March 2005 near Nias, an island off the coast of Sumatra. On the moment magnitude scale, this aftershock stood at 8.6, which ranks as the planet's sixth most powerful earthquake since 1900. In October 2005, scientists were still measuring aftershocks with magnitudes of 4 or 5.

Like the original earthquake, most of the aftershocks' epicenters were on the ocean floor rather than on islands. As a result, they have not caused much additional damage to people's homes or property. This is fortunate. Sometimes aftershocks can be as destructive as the original earthquake.

Region Affected by Aftershocks Following the 2004 Indian Ocean Earthquake

Andaman Islands

Thailand

Vietnam

Cambodia

South China Sea

Nicobar Islands

Malaysia

Simeulue

Nias

Equator

Sumatra

Borneo

Indian Ocean

Indonesia

Java

This hotel in Mexico City, Mexico, was devastated by an earthquake.

The earthquake that struck San Francisco, California, in 1906 destroyed this road and sidewalk. In parts of the city, gas mains broke, causing some fires that burned for four days.

More Disaster and Destruction

During a major earthquake, people fear for their lives. They do whatever they can to stay safe. When the shaking stops, people finally get a chance to look around. Often, what they see is devastating.

Buildings have collapsed and roads are destroyed. Power lines are down and telephones don't work. There is no way to check on family members and friends. People must prepare for the hard work it will take to rebuild their homes and their lives.

But the trouble may not be over. If the pipes carrying natural gas have been damaged, the gas may escape and catch on fire. If roads are blocked or destroyed, firefighters may have trouble reaching the scene. The flames can spread quickly and cause even more damage.

Earthquakes can also trigger other natural disasters. As you already know, the 2004 Indian Ocean earthquake caused a tsunami that affected many countries. As earthquakes shake the ground, they can also produce deadly landslides and avalanches.

This road in Nisqually, Washington, collapsed following a 2001 earthquake.

Did You Know?

A typical earthquake lasts under a minute.

On Shaky Ground

Iceland is an island located on top of the Mid-Atlantic Ridge. As you can see in the inset and background photos, the seafloor spreading occurring along the Mid-Atlantic Ridge is pulling the island apart. Scientists believe Iceland may be the site of a future earthquake.

Patterns of Quakes

An earthquake can occur anytime anyplace, but most happen along the edges of the plates in Earth's crust. As plates push against each other, pull apart, or slide past each other, pressure builds up. When the pressure gets too great, the rocks reach a breaking point.

Off the coasts of Washington and Oregon, the thin Juan de Fuca Plate is slowly subducting, or sliding below, the thicker North American Plate.

About 90 percent of all earthquakes occur along the edges of the Pacific Ocean, where thin ocean plates are sliding below thicker continental plates. As a thinner plate moves down into the mantle, the thicker plate crumples and buckles. Both motions cause pressure that can lead to earthquakes. This process is called **subduction**.

About 5 percent of all earthquakes strike in a zone that extends from the Mediterranean region through Turkey and Iran to northern India. In some areas of this collision belt, mountains are lifting upward as one continental plate is forced beneath another.

About 2 percent of all earthquakes occur along mid-ocean ridges, where **seafloor spreading** is forming new land. Even though the plates are moving apart, the surrounding rock is still under stress.

Most other earthquakes happen within the interiors of plates. Many of these, especially the ones that affect China,

occur where plate boundaries existed millions of years ago.

A small number of earthquakes are caused by humans. Building dams to create large reservoirs or drilling deep wells can put a lot of strain on the surrounding rock. Water can seep into crevices in the rock and weaken it. Eventually the rock cracks, shaking everything around it.

SMITHSONIAN LINK
Want to learn more about earthquakes?
Check out the Smithsonian's "Earthquakes" web page.
www.mnh.si.edu/earth/text/4_5_2_0.html

Doing More

No matter where you live, plate movements have shaped the land. What evidence of the crust's movement can you find in your town or in your state? Try asking a librarian or a geologist at a local college.

Where the Faults Lie

The fractures that form between shifting rock are called faults. This movement along a fault is called **offsetting**. Not all faults look the same. There are three basic kinds.

When rocks pull away from one another, the result is a normal fault. The land on one side of the break slips downward, so the land on the other side is noticeably higher. As the land or seafloor continues to move apart, a series of parallel normal faults may form. The result is called a rift valley. Rift valleys are currently forming in the Basin and Range region of the western United States. They are also responsible for the Sea of Cortez, or the Gulf of California, that separates Baja California from the rest of Mexico.

Normal fault

When rocks are pushed together, the rock on one side of the crack can ride up over the rock on the other side. The result is a thrust fault, or reverse fault. This is what usually happens in places where plates are colliding. Thrust fault activity occurred in the Appalachian Mountains millions of years ago.

Thrust fault

When the land on the sides of a crack moves in opposite directions or at different speeds, the result is a lateral fault, or transform fault. A long, wide fracture is visible on the ground, but the land on either side does not move up or down. The San Andreas Fault in California is one of the longest lateral faults in the world.

Lateral fault

The Basin and Range region of the western United States extends from eastern California to central Utah and from southern Idaho down into northern Mexico.

The Appalachian Mountains in the eastern United States were formed millions of years ago by thrust fault activity.

Animals and Earthquakes

We can't tell when an earthquake is about to strike, but some people think other animals can. In 1975, people in northeastern China noticed mice and rabbits leaving their burrows. Snakes came out of hibernation in the middle of winter. People in the area were concerned by the animals' strange behavior and decided to leave their homes. Shortly after they evacuated, a huge earthquake occurred. Did the animals know the quake was on its way? Most scientists say no, but a few aren't so sure. Whether the animals knew or not, following their lead saved many human lives. (But this method has led to some false alarms too, when people left their homes but no earthquake occurred.)

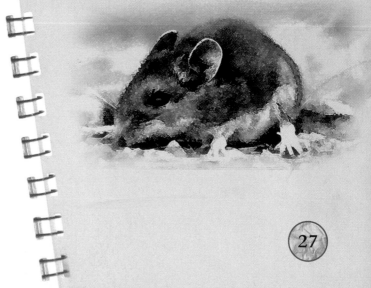

During the Loma Prieta earthquake in 1989, a portion of the San Francisco–Oakland Bay Bridge collapsed.

This aerial view shows a portion of the San Andreas Fault.

Did You Know?

In 1989, the Loma Prieta earthquake affected sports fans across North America by interrupting the World Series, which was being played in nearby San Francisco.

In Our Backyard: The San Andreas Fault

The San Andreas Fault is the largest fault in a complicated network of faults that slices through the rock near the California coast. In some places, the 800-mile-long zone of weakness is 10 miles deep and a few hundred feet wide.

The San Andreas Fault formed about 15 million years ago when the Pacific Plate and the North American Plate began moving in different directions. Today the Pacific Plate slowly slides northwest, while the North American Plate gradually grinds its way southwest.

Not all of the land along the San Andreas Fault moves at the same rate. In some areas, the land slowly creeps apart, a few inches each year. But in other areas, the land remains still for decades or even centuries. In these places, the rock on either side of the fault is locked together. Stress slowly builds up until the rock suddenly snaps, causing a major earthquake.

Since scientists began keeping records, three giant earthquakes have struck California. The Tejon Pass earthquake in 1857 had a magnitude of 8.25. The Owens Valley earthquake in 1872 had a magnitude of 7.6. The San Francisco quake of 1906, which had a magnitude of 8.25, killed as many as 3,000 people and destroyed much of San Francisco.

The most recent California quake to exceed 7 in magnitude struck Loma Prieta in October 1989. It killed 62 people and caused $6 billion in damage. Scientists predict that during the next 30 years, Californians have a 65 percent chance of experiencing an earthquake of magnitude 7 or greater.

SMITHSONIAN LINK
To find out more about North America's most famous fault, take a look at the Smithsonian's "San Andreas Fault" web page.
www.mnh.si.edu/earth/text/4_5_1_0.html

During the Loma Prieta earthquake, many buildings were destroyed in San Francisco's Marina District.

SEISMOGRAPHS · RECORDING THE EARTH'S SIGNALS

STATION LOCATION MAP ON WALL

MAMMOTH LAKES AREA

This scientist is checking one of the many seismographs at the U.S. Geological Survey's office in Menlo Park, California.

The Problem of Prediction

The scientists who study earthquakes are called **seismologists**. Using many different kinds of instruments, they monitor our planet's surface and interior for changes. Creepmeters and global positioning systems (GPS) placed on or near faults detect even the slightest movements in Earth's crust.

Seismographs located at monitoring stations all over the world measure the pattern of vibrations that spread through Earth when rocks in the crust slip and snap. They provide a visual record of an earthquake's P, S, Love, and Rayleigh waves. By comparing seismograph readings from several different sites, scientists can pinpoint the epicenter of any earthquake. They can also determine the earthquake's magnitude.

But seismologists are still unable to predict earthquakes. Because so many different factors determine the timing and strength of an earthquake, scientists' best information about future earthquakes comes from studying the patterns of the past. So even though scientists can't forecast earthquakes, they do know that during the last 1,200 years, the average time between major quakes along the San Andreas Fault zone has been 140 years. This information can help Californians prepare for the future.

That's Incredible!

Although the ancient Chinese had simple instruments that could detect earthquake vibrations, modern seismographs were invented in the late 1800s. By the early 1900s, scientists began noticing something surprising about P and S waves. As they radiate out from an earthquake's focus, they don't travel in straight lines or at a constant speed.

Scientists had trouble explaining these inconsistencies until they realized that different parts of Earth's interior must be made of different materials. Years of hard work eventually showed that our planet has four key layers—the crust, the mantle, the outer core, and the inner core. More recently seismologists have studied **seismic waves** (waves of movement created by earthquakes) to calculate how thick each layer is and to figure out what each layer is made of.

Preparing for Earthquakes

Scientists can't prevent earthquakes, and they can't predict exactly when or where they'll strike. But if cities and citizens are prepared, the amount of damage an earthquake causes can be greatly reduced.

In California and particularly in Japan, schools and businesses have regular earthquake drills. During the drills, people practice what to do in an emergency. They get under a sturdy piece of furniture or stand in a doorway. People should never run outside during an earthquake.

Earthquakes often affect power lines, gas mains, water supplies, and means of transportation. Families should have flashlights, helmets and sturdy shoes, a first aid kit, a fire extinguisher, bottled water, and canned food and a can opener. These items will help people walk to safety if it is possible, or survive where they are if that becomes necessary.

Town and city officials must think carefully about how an earthquake could affect their communities. New buildings and roads should be designed to limit damage. If possible, schools, hospitals, and fire stations should be built on stable land. Large buildings in danger zones should have flexible steel frames and deep, solid foundations. That way they can absorb and resist shaking. The buildings should be made of fire-resistant materials. All the furniture and heavy equipment inside should be bolted to floors or walls.

The Transamerica Pyramid in San Francisco, California, was designed to be twice as strong as building codes require. Its shape and structure help make it earthquake resistant.

Seeing Is Believing

In 1988, an earthquake with a magnitude of 6.8 struck Spitak, Armenia. It destroyed the city and killed more than 25,000 people. A year later, an earthquake with a magnitude of 7.1 struck San Francisco, California. Fewer buildings were destroyed and only 62 people died. Safer building practices made all the difference.

Michael Wise

Geologist/Curator, Department of Mineral Sciences,
National Museum of Natural History

What incident or person from your childhood influenced your decision to become a geologist?

I have always enjoyed science, even as a young boy. My early interest was not in rocks and minerals but in astronomy and chemistry. I never collected rocks as a child and did not know about geology until I was in college at the University of Virginia. It was there that I was first exposed to the fascinating discipline of geology. My college professor who taught me about minerals made the course very interesting.

How can kids get interested in your field?

Kids can get interested in rocks and minerals by just going outdoors, collecting as many different rocks and minerals as they can find. Look at them closely with a magnifying glass and see if you can see the different crystal shapes, colors, and sizes. You can join a local mineral club, where many people get together to share their experiences collecting rocks and minerals, display parts of their own collections, or take trips to mines and quarries where they actually collect their own samples.

What do you do most of the time? What do you do every day?

Most of the time I am in the laboratory doing research. Some days I may use special equipment to analyze the chemistry of rocks and minerals. Other times, I may be writing the results of my research.

Where and when do you do your research?

Most of my research is done in the museum. However, when I am in the field collecting rock samples, I go to Maine, Virginia, North Carolina, or California. Most of my fieldwork is in the spring and summer months.

What kind of education do you need?

To become a museum curator, you need to have a college education, typically a PhD, although some curators have only received a master's degree.

Do you travel in your job, and if so where?

As part of my job, I may travel across the United States to study the rocks that I am interested in learning about. Sometimes I present the results of my research at scientific meetings, which may be held in foreign countries such as Canada or Italy. Every year, my colleagues and I go to Denver, Colorado, and Tucson, Arizona, to attend two important gem and mineral shows. At these conventions, we buy many of our wonderful mineral specimens that can be found in our collection.

Is there something in your field you wish was studied more?

The rocks that I study are called pegmatites and they are very fascinating. They often have extremely large crystals and very complex mineral chemistry. They also are the source of many metals that are important for the manufacture of items that we use every day. Although they are so unusual, there are very few scientists who study them. More scientists are needed to figure out how these strange rocks form in nature.

What do you like most about your job?

The main thing that I like about my job is having the freedom to study whatever rocks interest me. My job allows me to be outdoors and to travel to different places. Buying gemstones and minerals for the museum is also a lot of fun. You get to see many different kinds of minerals and meet people from all over the world.

Who helps you do your job?

I am lucky enough to have a research assistant to help me analyze my rocks and minerals. She also travels with me in the field to collect the rocks and minerals that I need for my research.

The Rate of Recovery

When Mount St. Helens erupted in 1980, part of the mountain collapsed. The result was a massive avalanche and lateral eruption that flattened nearly 230 square miles of forest. Today plants and animals have begun to return to the area.

When Mount St. Helens erupted in 1980, it devastated the forest growing around the volcano [above left]. But by 1998, a variety of plants covered the mountainside [above right].

Quakes Before Eruptions

Earthquakes and volcanic eruptions can be closely related. Both are caused by the movement of Earth's plates. And in some cases, they occur at roughly the same time.

When a large supply of magma builds up, it puts tremendous pressure on the surrounding rock. All that stress can cause earthquakes. If magma accumulates beneath an existing volcano, some of it can erupt as lava or volcanic ash that helps build the volcano. In some cases magma may reach the surface along different fractures, forming a new volcano.

While some volcanoes produce more or less continuous relatively minor eruptions, others have powerful explosive eruptions that can devastate areas around the volcano. Scientists have learned that a series of small earthquakes can be a warning that a long-quiet volcano is about to erupt. This is what happened at Mount St. Helens in 1980.

Mount St. Helens, located in Washington State, is part of the Cascade Range. Before 1980, it had been quiet for more than a century. But scientists had evidence that the volcano had erupted at least 20 times in the last 4,500 years. They knew it was only a matter of time before it erupted again. About two months after scientists detected a rapid increase of minor earthquakes in the area, the volcano exploded violently.

In May 1980, Mount St. Helens had a major eruption for the first time since 1857. Scientists detected minor earthquakes shortly before the eruption, but they weren't expecting such a violent explosion. The eruption coincided with a magnitude 5.1 earthquake.

What Is a Volcano?

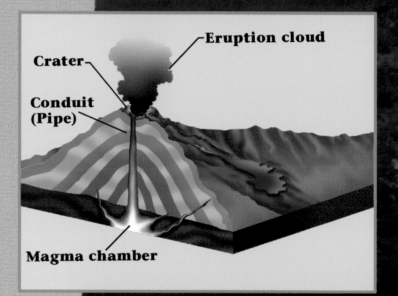

Crater

Eruption cloud

Conduit (Pipe)

Magma chamber

When you hear the word "volcano," you probably think of a giant, cone-shaped mountain. But volcanoes come in many shapes and sizes. Some are steep-sided, some are broad with gentle slopes, some are long cracks (or fissures), and others are actually large craters much wider than they are high.

A volcano's **crater** is the bowl-shaped opening at Earth's surface. When a volcano erupts, materials spill out of the crater. The **conduit**, or pipe, is a long, narrow tube that carries magma up to the crater. At the base of the vent is a **magma chamber**, a reservoir where fiery-hot gases and molten magma collect before an eruption.

Heat and pressure cause the molten material in a magma chamber to rise into any cracks or crevices it encounters. And when the heat and pressure inside a magma chamber is great enough, the material it holds rapidly rises up the conduit and the volcano erupts.

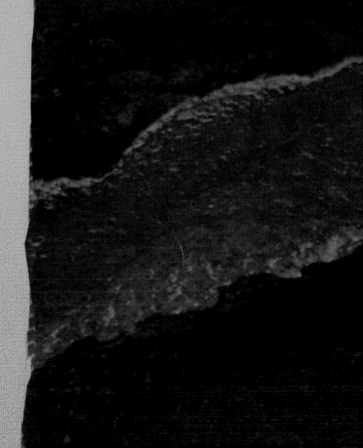

Lava: A Closer Look

When magma reaches Earth's surface, it is called lava. Lava flows can bury land and destroy plants, but they often move slowly. This usually gives people and other animals time to get out of the way. The surface of a lava flow can have three different kinds of textures. Aa lava is sticky and cools into a sharp and jagged surface. Pahoehoe is smooth and often cools into a surface that looks like masses of twisted rope. (Both "aa" and "pahoehoe" are Hawaiian words.) A third type of lava, called blocky lava, has a surface of overlapping blocks of different sizes.

When Mauna Loa last erupted in 1984, a river of pahoehoe lava slowly spread down the giant volcano's gentle slopes.

SMITHSONIAN LINK
Want to learn more about the anatomy of a volcano? Check out the Smithsonian's "Inside an Active Volcano" web page.
www.mnh.si.edu/earth/text/4_2_2_0.html

Lava, Ash, and Gas

Not all eruptions are the same. Sometimes a slow, steady stream of lava oozes out of a volcano for weeks, months, years, or even decades, possibly even forming a lake of molten lava. Other eruptions are more sudden and more explosive. The volcano erupts fiery fountains of lava into the sky and belches thick clouds of ash and steaming-hot gases. Sometimes a deadly mixture of rock, ash, and gases, called a pyroclastic flow, can rush down the volcano's slopes, destroying everything in its path.

Volcanic ash is made of tiny bits of lava that become solid as they hit the air. Some volcanic ash is a powdery dust so fine that some of it gets trapped in Earth's atmosphere. The rest of the ash drifts down and blankets the slopes of the volcano and surrounding areas.

Volcanic gas is made of steam and various chemicals. Carbon dioxide in the air can make it hard for people and other animals to breathe. Sulfur dioxide can mix with gases in the air to create acid rain. Fluorine and chlorine can damage the ozone layer, a thin layer of gases in Earth's atmosphere that blocks harmful rays from the sun.

Larger bits of volcanic rock are called **lapilli**. "Lapilli" is a Latin word meaning "small stones." These pebble-sized pieces of rock can rain down over a wide area of land.

The largest chunks of volcanic rock are called bombs. They can be as small as a baseball or as large as a car. Volcanic bombs can be very dangerous, but they usually don't travel far.

A plume of steam and gases rose high into the sky as Veniaminof, a volcano on the Alaskan Peninsula, erupted in 1984.

These huge volcanic bombs were ejected from *Pico de Teide*, a volcano on the Canary Islands, which are located off the coast of Spain.

Popocatepetl, a volcano in central Mexico, was named after an Aztec word that means "smoking mountain." During a 1997 eruption, it belched tons of ash and steam into the air.

Sizzling Sunsets

Following a volcanic eruption, people living nearby often enjoy beautiful sunsets. As the light of the sinking sun shines through bits of ash and dust in the air, the sky glows with brilliant pinks and reds. After very large eruptions, the sky at sunset may be red all over the world.

Kilauea in Hawaii has been erupting continuously since 1983. Lava shoots out of the volcano in short, frequent bursts.

Lava Locks

"Pele's hair" is the name used to describe long filaments of rock that form when thin, runny lava is caught by the wind and cools in long glassy strands before it hits the ground. If you saw Pele's hair, you'd probably never guess that it's a kind of volcanic rock.

Types of Eruptions

Some volcanic eruptions are deadly dangerous, while others may not affect humans at all. That's why scientists have come up with different categories, or types, of eruptions. Many of them are named for the places in which they were first described. To classify an eruption, scientists look at how violent it is and the kinds of materials thrown out.

In a Hawaiian eruption, lava fountains and lava rivers flow gently from the volcano and spread out over a wide area of land.

Strombolian eruptions are a bit more violent, but they are still not very dangerous. They produce tall fountains of lava almost continuously and may throw some ash and rock into the air.

Vulcanian eruptions are more violent and less frequent. They toss clouds of ash and lava bombs into the air. These big eruptions occur when gas builds up under thick, sticky lava. (Both Stromboli and Vulcano are volcanoes in Italy.)

Plinian eruptions are so fierce that they may empty the volcano's magma chamber, which can cause part of a volcanic mountain to collapse, forming a large depression called a caldera. Volcanoes of this type are named for the Roman naturalist Pliny the Elder, who died in an eruption of Vesuvius in A.D. 79.

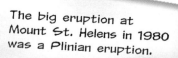

The big eruption at Mount St. Helens in 1980 was a Plinian eruption.

Mount Mazama's eruption that formed Crater Lake was many times more powerful than Mount St. Helen's eruption in 1980.

What's in a Name?

"Caldera" is the Spanish word for "cauldron," a large, old-fashioned pot used to cook soups and stews. A caldera's crater is shaped like a cauldron. Some people say that "caldera" can also be traced back to a Latin word that means "heat."

Mayon volcano in the Philippines is one of the most active composite volcanoes in the world. In this photo, lava blocks cascade down a gully on the steep cone.

Kinds of Volcanoes

Volcanoes come in a variety of shapes and sizes, from small hills to great mountains. What determines the structure and appearance of a volcano? The force with which it erupts and the kinds of materials it releases.

Repeated eruptions of runny, fluid lava flows form large volcanoes with broad bases and gently sloping sides.

More violent eruptions blast chunks of rock into the air. The rocks land near the crater, and the magma cools quickly. The result is steep-sided cinder cones only a few hundred feet high.

In contrast, composite volcanoes form by eruptions of both lava flows and explosive material. Over time, layer after layer of material builds up to form steep-sided, cone-shaped slopes.

Sometimes the lava is too sticky to flow out of a crater. When it cools, the molten material forms a steep-sided lava dome.

A caldera volcano has a broad, shallow crater. It is the result of a tremendous eruption that causes the volcano's summit to collapse. Some calderas have hills and mountains rising within them, which is a sign that more volcanic activity or deformation occurred after the initial collapse.

Sometimes very runny lava pours out of a long crack in Earth's surface and spreads out, rather than piling up to form a mountain. As lava spills out, a vast volcanic plateau, or plain, may form.

SMITHSONIAN LINK
To get a better sense of the shape and size of different kinds of volcanoes, check out the Smithsonian's "Volcano Profiles" web page.
www.mnh.si.edu/earth/text/4_2_1_0.html

In 1984, a 1,350-foot-tall fountain of lava erupted out of a fissure, or long crack, that formed at Hawaii's Kilauea volcano at the Pu'u O'o vent.

Strength and Size

There are roughly 500 active volcanoes that have erupted since people have been keeping written records. In any given year, between 50 and 60 volcanoes are active, but only a few cause major destruction to the surrounding land. (It may be that many more volcanoes erupt each year than we think. There are a lot of volcanoes on the ocean floor, but often we don't know when these erupt.)

To measure the strength and size of a volcano, scientists use a scale called the Volcanic Explosivity Index (VEI). It was developed in 1982 by American researcher Chris Newhall and British researcher Steve Self. Scientists use the VEI to estimate the size of eruptions that happened many years ago.

Like the moment magnitude scale used to rate earthquakes, the VEI evaluates the magnitude of a volcanic eruption. To assign a VEI value to an eruption, scientists consider the amount and type of material released, the height of the ash cloud, and other important factors.

The largest known eruptions have a VEI value of 8. One of them occurred about 640,000 years ago in what is now Yellowstone National Park. The other occurred about 73,000 years ago on Sumatra.

The largest historical eruption occurred in 1815, from Tambora volcano on the island of Sumbawa.

Volcanic Explosivity Index (VEI)

VEI	Example	Year	Documented Occurrences During the Past 10,000 Years
0	Masaya (Nicaragua)	1570	861
1	Poás (Costa Rica)	1991	1,113
2	Ruapehu (New Zealand)	1971	3,756
3	Nevado del Ruiz (Colombia)	1985	990
4	Pelée (West Indies)	1902	359
5	Mount St. Helens (United States)	1980	122
6	Krakatau (Indonesia)	1883	48
7	Tambora (Indonesia)	1815	7
8	Yellowstone (United States)	Pleistocene	0

Even an eruption with a VEI of 0 or 1 can do a great deal of damage. This photo shows fiery lava from a Hawaiian volcano.

Chip off the Old Block

During Krakatau's 1883 eruption, the summit of the volcano collapsed into the sea. In 1927, a new volcano rose in the same place. The Indonesians named it Anak Krakatau, which means "child of Krakatau."

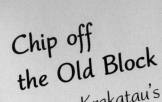

This drawing shows gases and ash erupting out of Krakatau during the devastating eruption of 1883. Ash falls can be seen on the right of the drawing.

During Mount Pinatubo's 1991 eruption, the lush, green forests growing on the volcano's slopes were scalded and buried by tons of ash.

Incredible Eruptions

Like an earthquake, the magnitude of a volcano eruption doesn't always match the amount of death and destruction it causes. A large eruption may not affect people much if no one lives nearby. On the other hand, a small eruption may be devastating if it occurs in an area that is heavily populated or if a river or valley channels lava, ash, or an avalanche toward a town or city.

The 1883 eruption of Krakatau in Indonesia registered a 6 on the VEI. It killed 36,000 people, making it the second deadliest on record. Most of the fatalities were due to the tsunamis generated by the eruption.

When Mount Pinatubo in the Philippines erupted in 1991, it was also given a VEI value of 6. But this time, scientists were able to anticipate the eruption. Even though the volcano had been inactive for more than six hundred years, several new behaviors, including minor local earthquakes, tremors, small steamy explosions, and unusual amounts of sulfur-dioxide gas, indicated restlessness. Shortly before the volcano erupted, 79,000 people evacuated the area. As a result, only 320 people died.

The Ten Deadliest Eruptions in Recorded History

Volcano	Location	Number of People Killed	VEI	Date A.D.
Tambora	Indonesia	60,000	7	1815
Krakatau	Indonesia	36,000	6	1883
Mount Pelée	Martinique	29,000	4	1902
Nevado del Ruiz	Colombia	23,000	3	1985
Unzen	Japan	14,300	2	1792
Kelut	Indonesia	10,000	5	1586
Santa Maria	Guatemala	10,000	6	1902
Laki	Iceland	9,350	6	1783
Kelut	Indonesia	5,500	4	1919
Galunggung	Indonesia	4,000	4	1822

After the Eruption

Ash and Airplanes

In 1982, a jet airplane flew near Indonesia's Galunggung volcano shortly after an eruption. Ash from the eruption clogged all four engines, and the plane lost nearly five miles of elevation before the pilot was able to restart the engines. It was a close call!

Because the ash particles were so tiny and so spread out, the pilot couldn't see them. But when engines sucked in the ash, it melted and then clogged the fuel lines. It also caused other mechanical problems. In recent years, similar incidents have damaged more than 60 airplanes. Luckily, none of the planes have crashed. Still, aviation authorities are searching for ways to decrease the risk posed by volcanic ash. Today they work with scientists to track ash clouds and plan airplane routes around them.

This photo shows ash spewing from Galunggung volcano during its 1982 eruption. Even as the ash swiftly spread out with high-altitude winds, there was still a major threat to airplanes flying in the area.

The Trouble Continues

Explosive volcanic eruptions can wipe out forests and villages. Sometimes they even destroy entire islands. But these aren't the only kinds of damage an eruption can cause.

Many volcanoes take the form of cone-shaped mountains. Some are so tall that their peaks are covered with snow and ice all year long. The tremendous heat of an eruption can melt the ice and snow, triggering mudslides and avalanches. This is what happened at Colombia's Nevado del Ruiz in 1985.

The Nevado del Ruiz eruption was relatively small, registering only a 3 on the volcanic explosivity index. But the snow it melted caused a mudflow that destroyed several towns and killed 23,000 people. It is the fourth deadliest eruption on record.

As materials from a volcano rain down on the land, they can clog rivers and cause flooding. If the area receives heavy rains, layers of ash may turn to mud that flows down volcanic slopes. This is what happened at Mount Pinatubo following its 1991 eruption. Even though only 320 people died during the eruption, a series of mudflows killed an additional 600 people. One particularly severe mudflow left 100,000 people homeless.

Following the 1991 eruption of Mount Pinatubo in the Philippines, the area experienced heavy rains and flooding. Thick, muddy flows of ash and water buried many buildings, including this school.

What's the Weather?

During a powerful eruption, a volcano shoots out molten material of all sizes. The force of gravity quickly pulls lava bombs to the ground. Within a few hours, most of the lapilli rain down over the surrounding land. But some ash is so fine and lightweight that it can be thrust many miles into Earth's atmosphere. It may stay there for days, weeks, or even months.

The ash doesn't remain confined to the area of the eruption. As time passes, it spreads farther and farther. Satellite images showed that just 18 days after the 1991 eruption of Mount Pinatubo, ash particles had traveled halfway around the world.

During violent eruptions, volcanoes may blast chunks of hardened lava high into the air. Large pieces [top], called bombs, come in all shapes and sizes. Gravel-sized chunks [bottom] are called lapilli.

After two months, a thin cloud of ash and aerosols circled the entire planet.

Weather records from the past suggest that violent volcanic eruptions can affect weather patterns worldwide. The 1815 eruption of Tambora in Indonesia was the deadliest eruption recorded since people began keeping written records. It thrust 1.7 million tons of ash into the air. Because the debris blocked some of the sun's rays, the following winter was especially severe all over the world. And the summer of 1816 was the coolest on record. In North America and Europe, some people called 1816 "the year without a summer."

Volcanic ash is so lightweight that it can easily spread hundreds of miles before it falls to the ground. This farmer's field in Connell, Washington, was blanketed with ash following the 1980 eruption of Mount St. Helens.

Did You Know?

Ice or raindrops slowly build up on bits of dust and debris in the air. When a raindrop gets heavy enough, it falls to the ground. When massive amounts of ash suddenly enter the air, raindrops can form more easily. Past weather records confirm that the areas surrounding volcanoes often receive more rain than normal following an explosive eruption.

How the West Was Made

At one time, the western edge of North America lay east of the Rocky Mountains. But as a series of thin ocean plates crashed into the thick, sturdy North American Plate, the small landmasses they carried became part of our continent. The Rockies, the Cascade Range, and the Sierra Nevada all contain evidence of ancient collisions.

The mighty Rocky Mountains are solid and still today, but they are the result of a violent collision that happened millions of years ago.

54

Ring of Fire

Volcanoes are not spread evenly over Earth's surface. Like earthquakes, they are most common along the edges of the plates.

So many volcanoes rise along the edges of the Pacific Plate that the area is sometimes called "the Ring of Fire." Along these edges, Earth's plates are colliding and one is diving down into Earth. As the lower plate descends, huge quantities of new magma are created. Some of that magma rises to the Earth's surface and erupts from a volcano.

Deep ocean trenches mark the boundary between two subducting plates. It is the place where the thinner ocean plate slips beneath the thicker continental plate. The Mariana Trench, located off the coast of Guam and the Mariana Islands, is the deepest area of the oceans.

SMITHSONIAN LINK
For more information about the location of Earth's active volcanoes, take a look at the Smithsonian's "Tracking Volcanoes" web page.
www.mnh.si.edu/earth/text/4_2_3_0.html

Tori-shima, Japan, is located along the western edge of the Ring of Fire. The volcano last erupted in 2002.

At 10,778 feet, Mount Baker is the tallest mountain in northern Washington. Like Mount St. Helens, it is one of many active volcanoes in the Cascade Range.

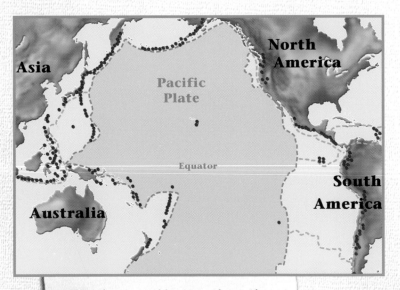

The dots on this map show the location of volcanoes. Notice how they form a ring along the edges of the Pacific Plate.

Mid-Ocean Ridges

Volcanoes also form in places where plates are moving apart. As the plates travel away from each other, magma rises to the surface and slowly spills out. Where are these volcanoes located? Most are deep below the ocean's surface.

If you could look at a map of ocean floors all over the world, you'd see a network of massive ridges, such as the Mid-Atlantic Ridge, the East Pacific Rise, and the Southwest Indian Ridge, that crisscross Earth's surface, like the stitching on a baseball.

In the center of the ridges are deep cracks that pass through the crust and penetrate the mantle. Magma moves up into the cracks and, over time, rises to the surface. It flows out of the cracks and onto the seafloor. As soon as the lava comes into contact with a deep sea's frigid waters, it cools quickly and forms new seafloor. So as Earth's plates slowly separate, magma fills in the gaps. As time passes, the oceans grow wider and continents move farther apart.

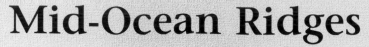

Juan de Fuca Ridge

East Pacific Rise

Pacific Antarctic Ridge

Chile Ridge

Heated water is belched out of an undersea volcano. When the hot water comes into contact with chilly ocean water, the minerals fall to the seafloor and form new layers of rock.

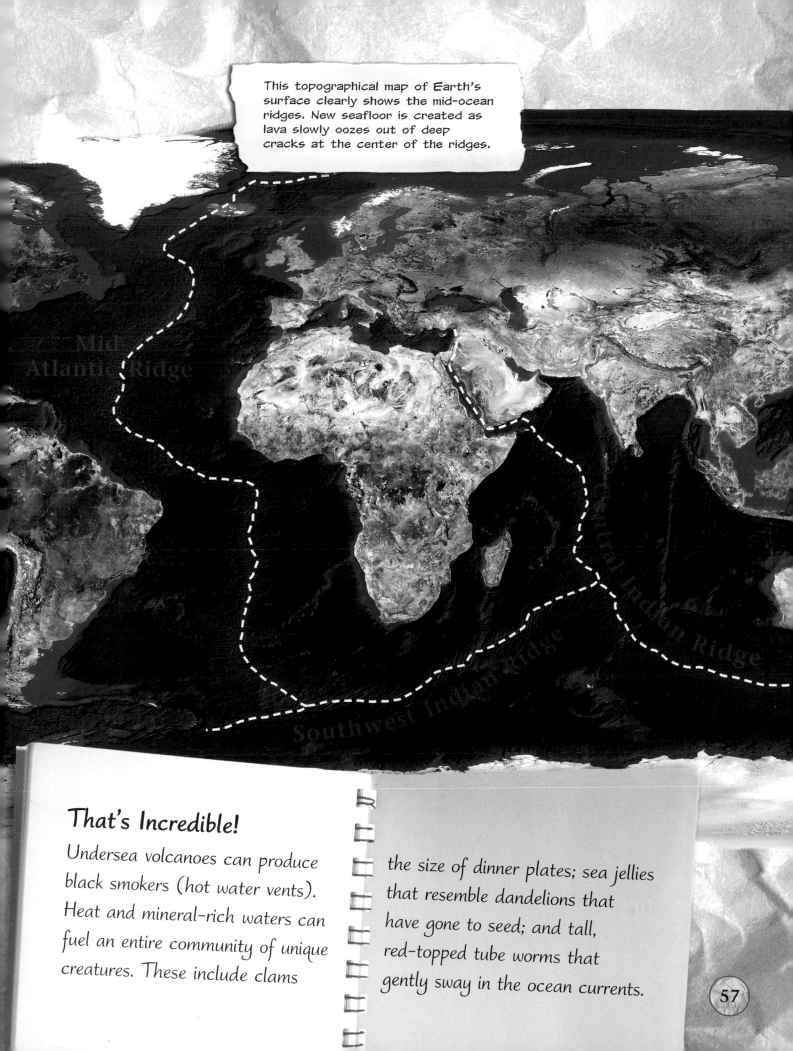

This topographical map of Earth's surface clearly shows the mid-ocean ridges. New seafloor is created as lava slowly oozes out of deep cracks at the center of the ridges.

Mid Atlantic Ridge

Central Indian Ridge

Southwest Indian Ridge

That's Incredible!

Undersea volcanoes can produce black smokers (hot water vents). Heat and mineral-rich waters can fuel an entire community of unique creatures. These include clams the size of dinner plates; sea jellies that resemble dandelions that have gone to seed; and tall, red-topped tube worms that gently sway in the ocean currents.

When viewed from space, the Hawaiian Islands (below), formed by volcanoes, look like a chain of emeralds in the sea. The island of Hawaii, the "Big Island," is on the right.

Hot Spots

Not all volcanoes form along the edges of plates. The Hawaiian Islands are a perfect example. They are located smack dab in the middle of the Pacific Plate.

These islands formed as lava slowly leaked out of a **hot spot**—a place where magma rises through Earth's crust in the middle of a plate—and piled up over millions of years. Eventually, the pile became tall enough to poke above the surface of the ocean and form an island.

Hot spots do not move, but the land above them does. As a result, we can see the trails of the islands or mountains they leave behind. The same hot spot is responsible for all the Hawaiian Islands.

Scientists have identified about fifty hot spots all over the world. While many are located below the seafloor, like the Hawaiian hot spot, others are centered below land. One of these is the Yellowstone hot spot. It is located beneath Yellowstone National Park, which occupies the northwest corner of Wyoming and stretches into Idaho and Montana. Heat from the Yellowstone hot spot fuels the park's world-famous network of hot springs and geysers, including Old Faithful.

Hawaii's Mauna Loa volcano (above) is located almost directly over a hot spot. The hot spot below much of Yellowstone National Park (left) fuels dozens of geysers and hot springs.

A Hot Spot Gone Cold

The Glass House Mountains in Queensland, Australia, are the remains of a mountain chain created by a hot spot long ago. Twenty-five million years of wind and rain have eroded the softer rock, leaving only the volcanoes' hard central cores.

SMITHSONIAN LINK
Want to learn more about hot spots? Take a look at the Smithsonian's "Above Hot Spots" web page.
www.mnh.si.edu/earth/text/4_2_5_0.html

In Our Backyard: Western United States

The west coast of North America lies along the eastern edge of the Ring of Fire, so it's no surprise that the area is home to many volcanoes.

The Cascade Range, which includes Mount St. Helens, extends from northern California through Oregon and Washington and into British Columbia, Canada. The eruptions along this range are fueled by magma that forms as the tiny Juan de Fuca and Gorda plates slide under the thicker North American Plate. (The Gorda Plate also has another side that scrapes past the Pacific Plate, along an offshoot of the San Andreas Fault.)

Another chain of volcanoes stretches along the southern coast of Alaska and across the Aleutian Islands. Volcanoes such as Augustine, Novarupta, Redoubt, and Veniaminof erupt as the Pacific Plate subducts under the North American Plate.

Following six hours of mild earthquake activity, Mount Augustine in Alaska erupted violently on January 11, 2006.

Did You Know?

One of the largest eruptions along the Cascade Range occurred about 6,800 years ago at Mount Mazama. The crystal blue waters of Crater Lake in Oregon fill a deep caldera created by the eruption. Wizard Island is a volcanic cone that formed about 4,600 years ago on the far western side of the lake.

Igneous Rock

As soon as lava hits air or water, it begins to cool. Depending on the size of an eruption, lava may take anywhere from a few minutes to thousands of years to harden. Then it becomes igneous rock, such as basalt or rhyolite. The word "igneous" comes from the Latin word "igneus," meaning "burning."

There are many different kinds of volcanic rock. If lava cools very quickly, it can form shiny volcanic glass, such as obsidian or tachylyte. If lava is full of air bubbles as it cools, it forms pumice. The tiny holes in pumice make it the lightest rock on Earth. It can even float on water. Cinder is heavier than pumice, but it too has holes that mark ancient gas bubbles.

Kimberlite is a volcanic rock that contains chunks of many different minerals, including garnets and, sometimes, diamonds. When this deep-seated magma is forced up from Earth's interior, it carries the minerals along with it.

Lava often cools from the outside in because the outer edges are exposed to the cool air.

The great moai statues on Easter Island are made of basalt.

Pumice forms when a volcano spews lava as a frothy mixture full of gas bubbles. The holes in pumice make it so lightweight that the rock can often float in water.

Haunting Rock

The world-famous moai statues on Easter Island in the Pacific Ocean were carved from basalt, Earth's most common igneous rock. Native people created the giant statues more than four hundred years ago.

Native American peoples used another igneous rock, obsidian, to make tools and weapons, such as arrowheads. Obsidian flakes easily and breaks in a way that forms sharp edges. Igneous rocks are found in close association with ore deposits, which modern society depends upon.

SMITHSONIAN LINK
Want to learn more about how crystals form? Take a look at the Smithsonian's "Crystal Growth" web page.
www.mnh.si.edu/earth/text/2_2_2_0.html

The Rock Cycle

As magma cools to create new igneous rock, other kinds of rocks are slowly being destroyed. You may think rock is indestructible; but over time, wind, water, and ice can break it down. Crashing ocean waves, raging rivers, whipping winds, and galloping glaciers can wear away, or **erode**, even the hardest rock.

Rock can also be broken down when plant roots grow into cracks or crevices, when acid rain and snow fall, when living creatures release chemicals from their bodies, and by repeated freezing and thawing. This is called **weathering**. Have you ever seen a boulder that looked like it had mysteriously split in half? The split was probably the result of weathering.

As rock breaks down and wears away, the tiny pieces may be picked up by rivers and streams. Eventually, these sediments travel all the way to the ocean. Over time, layers of sediments build up on the ocean floor and form **sedimentary rock**.

As Earth's plates move, some of the sedimentary rock becomes part of the land. When the layers shift and compress, the sedimentary rock may be exposed to tremendous heat and pressure. Over millions of years, the sedimentary rock may change into **metamorphic rock**. Or the rock may be pulled into the mantle and melt to produce magma. Eventually, some of that magma will cool to form still more igneous rock.

See for Yourself

The next time you visit the seashore or a large lake, pick up some pebbles along the beach. The edges of the beach pebbles will probably be round and smooth because water has worn them down. This is good evidence of erosion at work.

SMITHSONIAN LINK
Want to learn more about rocks and minerals? You can get started at the Smithsonian's "Three Rocks and Their Minerals" web page.
www.mnh.si.edu/earth/text/3_1_2_1.html

As flowing lava comes into contact with the chilly sea, it cools and hardens to form new rock. At the same time, crashing waves nearby wear away bits of the shoreline (background). In a New England forest, repeated freezing and thawing have caused this boulder to split in half (above).

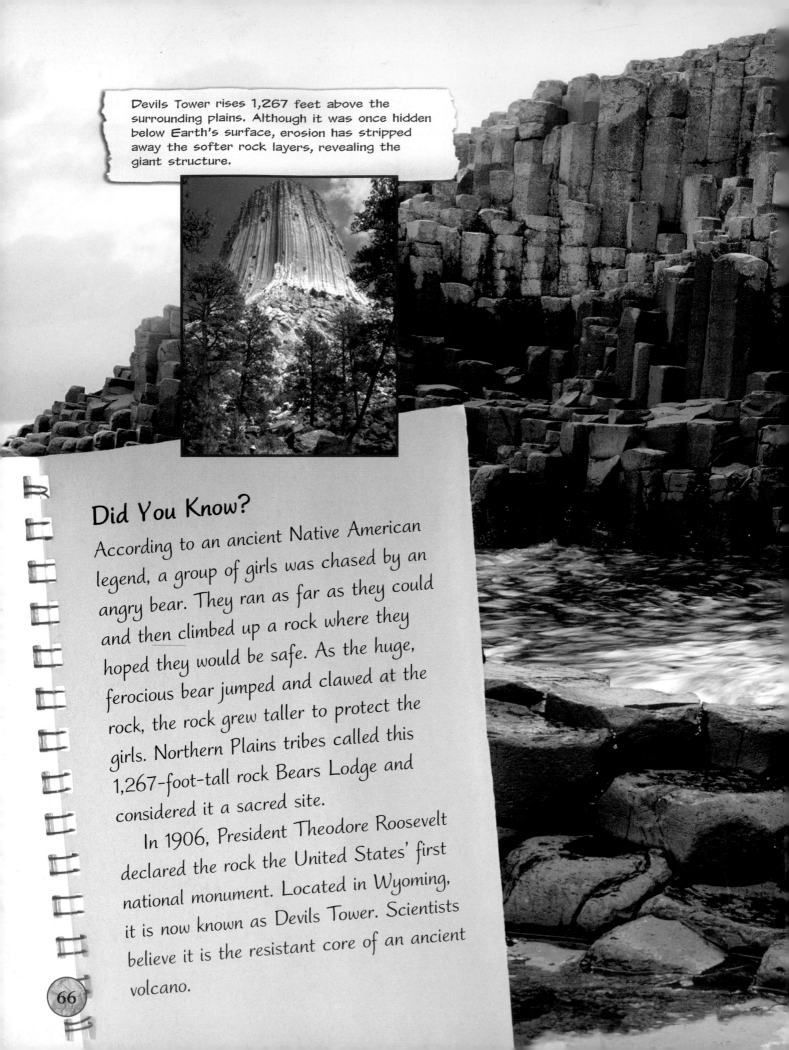

Devils Tower rises 1,267 feet above the surrounding plains. Although it was once hidden below Earth's surface, erosion has stripped away the softer rock layers, revealing the giant structure.

Did You Know?

According to an ancient Native American legend, a group of girls was chased by an angry bear. They ran as far as they could and then climbed up a rock where they hoped they would be safe. As the huge, ferocious bear jumped and clawed at the rock, the rock grew taller to protect the girls. Northern Plains tribes called this 1,267-foot-tall rock Bears Lodge and considered it a sacred site.

In 1906, President Theodore Roosevelt declared the rock the United States' first national monument. Located in Wyoming, it is now known as Devils Tower. Scientists believe it is the resistant core of an ancient volcano.

Volcanic Landscapes

Igneous rocks, such as basalt and obsidian, are the most common rocks in Earth's crust. Many of the world's mountains have formed as lava spilled out of the crust, cooled, hardened, and slowly piled up. Igneous rocks also lie beneath the floor of all the oceans.

As rain and water slowly eroded ancient igneous mountains, some of the most unusual and most beautiful structures on Earth appeared. Many ancient legends try to explain how Giant's Causeway in Northern Ireland formed. Today we know these steplike columns are the result of a thick lava flow that cooled slowly and formed a network of cracks. As the sea slowly eroded the basalt structure, rock came away along the cracks, creating blocks that look like a huge staircase. Le Puy-de-Dôme in France is the hard central core of what was once a volcano. The softer surrounding rocks have been slowly eroded over time.

Obsidian is usually found in small amounts. But giant rock formations such as the Glass Buttes in Oregon and the volcanic domes inside the Mono Craters and Inyo Craters in California are made entirely of obsidian.

As igneous rock breaks down, tiny bits and pieces wash into the plains near the base of volcanic mountains. Because igneous rock contains many of the nutrients plants need to grow, the soil around a volcano is often perfect for farming.

Giant's Causeway on the northern coast of Northern Ireland formed 62 to 65 million years ago, during the early Tertiary period.

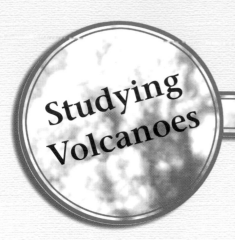

Alive or Not?

Because the forces that cause volcanoes are at work deep below Earth's surface, it's hard to know when a volcano will erupt or how dangerous the eruption will be. Some volcanoes erupt gently but continuously. Others explode violently every few years or every few centuries. And some volcanoes may alternate between minor eruptions and major eruptions.

Volcanologists classify volcanoes based on their history of eruptions. An active volcano has erupted within the last 10,000 years and is expected to erupt again in the future. There are 1,500 volcanoes on Earth identified as having erupted during this interval and only about 15 that are well known for erupting nearly all the time. Volcanoes can remain quiet for long periods and then resume erupting.

Many volcanoes that have not erupted during recorded history are likely to erupt again. These volcanoes can be particularly dangerous, as people living nearby may incorrectly consider them to be safe.

How do scientists determine whether a volcano is active or not? They study them. They scramble up steep slopes and clamber into craters to observe the structure of volcanoes and collect rock samples. Sometimes they set up equipment that measures earthquake activity and detects temperature changes inside the crater. Then they return to their labs and spend many hours analyzing their data.

Most of the volcanoes of the world have never been seen because they are on the seafloor. Scientists know that these volcanoes are frequently active, but they have rarely seen one erupt.

These scientists are studying a spot, or fumerole, where the escaping gas is depositing native sulfur, the yellow crusted material. The data they collect may help them develop new strategies for predicting eruptions.

Did You Know?

Kilauea in Hawaii is one of the most active—and most studied—volcanoes in the world. It has erupted without significant pause for several decades.

Predicting Eruptions

Before an eruption, volcanologists pay close attention to earthquake activity, ground movement, and the release of gases. When a volcano erupts, they monitor it closely. They film lava flows and gas clouds from a safe distance.

During gentle eruptions, a few scientists occasionally put on bulky, heat-resistant suits and study the lava up close. They measure its temperature and observe how it cools. When the volcano settles down, they may don hard hats and special gloves and shoes and hike around the slopes and craters.

The goal of this work is to predict the timing and severity of eruptions, so people can be evacuated when necessary. While scientists still have much to learn, they are beginning to see signs and identify patterns that can help save lives.

As you already learned, an increase in earthquake activity can be a sign that a volcano is about to erupt. If scientists' measurements of a volcano show that it is swelling, magma may be gathering near the surface. Scientists also watch for increases in gas emissions, especially ones that include large amounts of sulfur dioxide. If scientists see all three of these signs, it is likely that an eruption is about to occur.

As soon as Mount Talang in Indonesia started to rumble, scientists advised the people living on the volcano's slopes to evacuate.

Since Mount St. Helens erupted in 1980, scientific study about volcanic activity has led to many accurate predictions of impending eruptions around the world.

That's Incredible!

Volcanologists are not the only scientists who help us understand the power of volcanoes. In 2005, scientists studying the ocean reported that large volcanic eruptions can temporarily lower sea levels slightly. Ash spewed from major eruptions cools land and water all over the world. These climate changes can last years or even decades. Sea levels fall because cold water takes up less space than warm water. Falling sea levels happened after the 1963 eruption of Mount Agung in Indonesia and in 1991 after the eruption of Mount Pinatubo in the Philippines.

Volcanoes on Other Worlds

This computer-generated image of Olympus Mons was created using data collected by the *Viking* spacecraft.

Up Close and Personal

In the late 1960s and 1970s, a dozen American astronauts visited Earth's moon. Most of them were pilots, but Harrison "Jack" Schmitt was a geologist—a scientist who studies rocks and rock formations to understand how a moon or planet formed and changed over time. During his Apollo 17 mission, Schmitt observed some of the moon's volcanic surface features firsthand. Later, he described what he saw to other scientists.

Earth is not the only planet with volcanoes. Mars is home to several huge volcanoes that have been extinct for millions of years. The biggest, Olympus Mons, is wider than all the Hawaiian volcanoes put together. Astronauts discovered that Earth's moon also shows evidence of ancient volcanic activity.

Venus has volcanoes, too, and some scientists believe a few may still be active. The surface of our closest neighboring planet is 90 percent basalt, and its surface shows signs of recent lava flows. The tremendous amount of sulfur dioxide in Venus's atmosphere and frequent lightning may be signs of ongoing eruptions.

In 1979, *Voyager 2* captured images of an erupting volcano on Io, one of Jupiter's moons. Scientists estimate that plumes of lava and gas were thrust nearly 175 miles above Io's surface. Nearly 20 years later, images returned by *Galileo* showed more dramatic evidence of volcanic activity on Io. The eruptions are a sign that Io has a molten core, but the eruptions aren't related to the movement of plates. Scientists think they are caused by the gravitational pull of Jupiter and the planet's other large moons.

In 1989, *Voyager 2* made another startling discovery—evidence of volcanoes on Triton, one of Neptune's moons. More recently, the *Cassini-Huygens* spacecraft returned images of volcanoes on Titan, the largest moon of Saturn.

SMITHSONIAN LINK
Visit the National Museum of Natural History's "The Solar System" exhibition online.
www.mnh.si.edu/earth/text/5_0_0.html

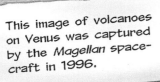
This image of volcanoes on Venus was captured by the *Magellan* spacecraft in 1996.

Andrew Johnston

Geographer, National Air and Space Museum

Why did you become a geographer?

Being a geographer allows me to investigate a wide range of questions: How do lava flows behave, how does Earth's surface change, how does Earth compare to other planets? I can't remember a time when I wasn't interested in those kinds of questions. This career was a natural choice.

What do you do most of the time?

I work with satellite images on computers, creating museum exhibits, programs, and books. I also travel to various places to perform scientific fieldwork, which includes camping and working outdoors.

What skills and tools do you need to do your job?

I use computers, mapping and image processing software, GPS survey equipment, and image data from satellites to understand Earth's surface. Sometimes it can be complicated, but just about anyone can learn how to use these tools.

What are the most important qualities for an expert in your field?

The important things are curiosity, creativity, and an ability to think logically. It's also essential to have writing and speaking skills. The ability to memorize lots of facts is *not* important.

What other experts might you talk with?

I work with experts in geology and geophysics to help understand volcanoes. I occasionally work with anthropologists and biologists on other research projects.

Do you need any special training (apart from a college education) for your job?

Much of the work involves computer programs, so it is helpful to understand how these programs work. Training in specific software is not always necessary, however. You can teach yourself to use just about any kind of computer program. That's how I learned.

What new technology has helped you most with your job?

Over the last 10 years the Global Positioning System (GPS) has changed the way we do fieldwork. We use advanced GPS units to perform surveys that are accurate to a few centimeters. We use these tools to measure the shape and size of features such as lava flows and sand dunes.

Do you travel in your job, and if so where?

Part of my job involves scientific fieldwork, and it takes me to many destinations. I've worked extensively in Kenya, Peru, and Egypt, and in Hawaii, New Mexico, the Mojave Desert, and other places in the United States.

Is there something in your field you wish everyone knew about?

Being a geographer is about understanding why things are located *where* they are located. Geographers also study the connections between humans and the physical world. Geographers attempt to answer questions such as: Why do certain lava flows move the way they do? What makes some places lush and green and other places dry? Why are cities built in certain locations?

What do you like most about your job?

I love my job because it allows me to study and answer big questions about the natural world. I enjoy reaching out to people to tell them about what we do. These are the kind of things I've been interested in since I was a child.

Glossary

core—The innermost part of Earth, made up of the metals nickel and iron. The inner core is solid, and the outer core is liquid.

crater—A bowl-shaped depression created when magma breaks through the surface, or when collapse occurs.

crust—The outer layer of Earth. A zone composed of tectonic plates that move.

earthquake—Vibrations that radiate through Earth's interior when the plates that make up Earth's surface collide or slip past each other.

epicenter—The point on Earth's surface that is directly above the focus of an earthquake.

erode—To slowly wear away rock over time by the action of wind, water, or glaciers.

fault—A crack that forms in zones or areas that are weak as rocks shift in Earth's crust.

focus—The place from which earthquake waves radiate.

geologist—A scientist who studies rocks, ores, and minerals. Some geologists study rocks to learn how Earth has changed over time. Others study how rocks are made and their scientific properties.

hot spot—A place where magma rises into or through Earth's crust in the middle of a plate.

intensity—A measure of the damage done by an earthquake.

lapilli—Pebble-size bits of rock that spew from a volcano.

lava—Magma that has been forced up to Earth's surface.

magma—Hot, molten rock that may contain crystals, chunks of unmelted rock, and gases, including steam or water vapor. Magma makes up part of Earth's mantle.

magma chamber—The area beneath a volcano where magma collects before an eruption.

magnitude—A measure of the amount of energy released by an earthquake or volcanic eruption.

mantle—The layer of Earth between the crust and outer core. It is made of hot

rock that can contain some magma.

metamorphic rock—Rock that forms when heat or pressure or both change the minerals within igneous rock, sedimentary rock, or another kind of metamorphic rock.

offset—The amount of movement along a fault. This is one of the features that geologists can reconstruct after some large earthquakes, and it can help confirm an earthquake's magnitude.

plate—One of the large slabs of rock that make up Earth's crust.

rift—A crack that forms in Earth's crust as plates move apart.

seafloor spreading—The process that occurs when Earth's plates move apart, creating a rift on the floor of the ocean.

sedimentary rock—A kind of rock that forms as layers of mud, clay, and tiny rocks build up over time.

seismic—About or related to earthquakes.

seismologist—A scientist who studies earthquakes.

subduction—When one plate moves under another plate.

tsunami (pronounced sue-NAHM-ee)—Dangerous, powerful waves that travel rapidly through water and are created by geological activity beneath a body of water.

vent—The pipe that connects a volcano's magma chamber to its crater.

volcano—A place on a planet's surface where molten rock, gases, and ash erupt through the crust on land or the seafloor.

volcanologist—A scientist who studies volcanoes.

weathering—The breaking down of rock by plant roots, by repeated freezing and thawing, and by other natural causes.

More to See and Read

WEBSITES

There are links to many wonderful web pages in this book. But the web is constantly growing and changing, so we cannot guarantee that the sites we recommend will be available. If the site you want is no longer there, you can always find your way to plenty of information about earthquakes and volcanoes and a great learning experience through the main Smithsonian website: www.si.edu.

Mount St. Helens VolcanoCam
www.fs.fed.us/gpnf/volcanocams/msh

San Andreas Fault
http://pubs.usgs.gov/gip/earthq3/intro.html

Smithsonian Institution Global Volcanism Program
www.volcano.si.edu

This Dynamic Planet
www.minerals.si.edu/tdpmap

Understanding Earthquakes
www.crustal.ucsb.edu/ics/understanding

Volcano World
http://volcano.und.edu

World-Wide Earthquake Locator
http://tsunami.geo.ed.ac.uk/local-bin/quakes/mapscript/home.pl

SUGGESTED READING

Don't Know Much About Planet Earth by Kenneth C. Davis

Earth edited by James Luhr

Earthquakes and Volcanoes by Lin Sutherland

Eyewitness Volcano & Earthquake by Susanna Van Rose

Forces of Nature: The Awesome Power of Volcanoes, Earthquakes, and Tornadoes by Catherine O'Neill Grace

Into the Volcano: A Volcano Researcher at Work by Donna O'Meara

When the Earth Moves by Sandra Downs

Index